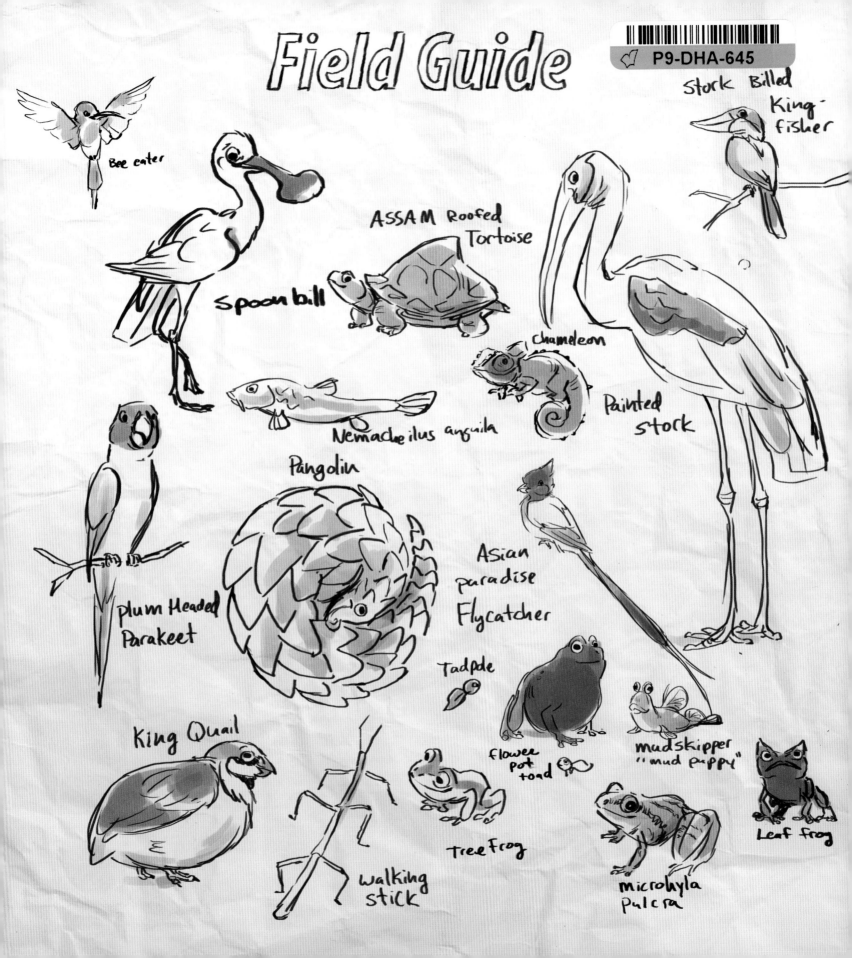

For Marsha,
the Scariest Thing
in the Jungle.

—DDjr

immedium
inspiring a world of imagination

Immedium, Inc.
P.O. Box 31846
San Francisco, CA 94131
www.immedium.com

First hardcover edition published 2013.

Edited by Tracy Swedlow
Book design by Erica Loh Jones

Printed in Malaysia
10 9 8 7 6 5 4 3 2 1

Library of Congress Cataloging-in-
Publication Data

Derrick, David G., 1978-author, illustrator.
I'm the scariest thing in the jungle! /
by David Derrick.
—First hardcover edition.
pages cm
Summary: "A bengal tiger cub and
little crocodile vie for bragging rights
about who is the scariest animal in their Indian jungle"—Provided by
publisher.
ISBN 978-1-59702-087-9 (hardcover)
[1. Bengal tiger—Fiction. 2. Tigers—Fiction. 3. Crocodiles—Fiction. 4.
Jungle animals—Fiction. 5. Fear—Fiction.] I. Title. II. Title: I am the
scariest thing in the jungle!
PZ7.D4465Im 2013
[E]—dc23
2013010351
ISBN: 978-1-59702-087-9

I'm the SCARIEST THING in the Jungle!

Written and Illustrated by
David G. Derrick, Jr.

immedium
www.immedium.com
San Francisco. CA

In the wilds of India,
there are two animals who
frighten all others...

The mighty tiger...

and the great crocodile.

"BOO!"

"I'm the **SCARIEST THING** in the jungle!"

Your crackled skin is about as
scary as an old log.

I'm twice as scary as you 'cause
I can stalk in the water, see in the dark,
and vanish in the grass,

so I'm the scariest
thing in the jungle!

You can't be serious.
When I'm in the water
nobody DARES get a drink.
I REIGN over the river.
I've got tough armored
skin, cold steely eyes,
and am near invisible, so

I'm the SCARIEST THING in the jungle!

Ha! You can't climb.
You can barely waddle up
a riverbank
I can attack from the trees,
stalk in the water,
see in the dark,
and vanish in the grass,
so
I'm the

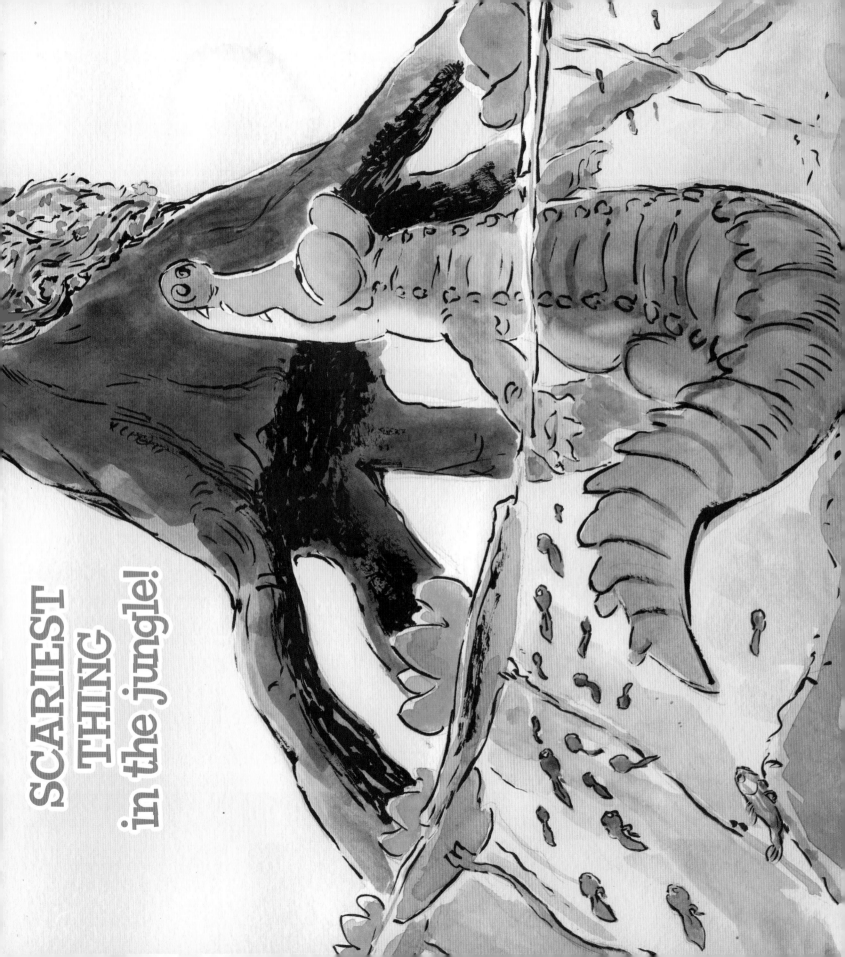

SCARIEST THING in the jungle!

Check out my mouth. See those? I've got the fiercest teeth you've ever seen. I reign over the river. I've got tough armored skin, cold steely eyes, and am near invisible, so I'm the **scariest thing in the jungle!**

DEADLY? Those bitty toothpicks aren't good for much more than snapping at minnows. My killer canines could crack a coconut!

sproing!

Besides I have claws that are always sharp. I can attack from the trees, stalk in the water, see in the dark, and vanish in the grass, so I'm the scariest thing in the jungle!

ARE NOT!
I can chew up boulders
for breakfast and
take down five rhinos, four gaur,
and a chital before lunch!

Sounds BIG...

and
SCARY!

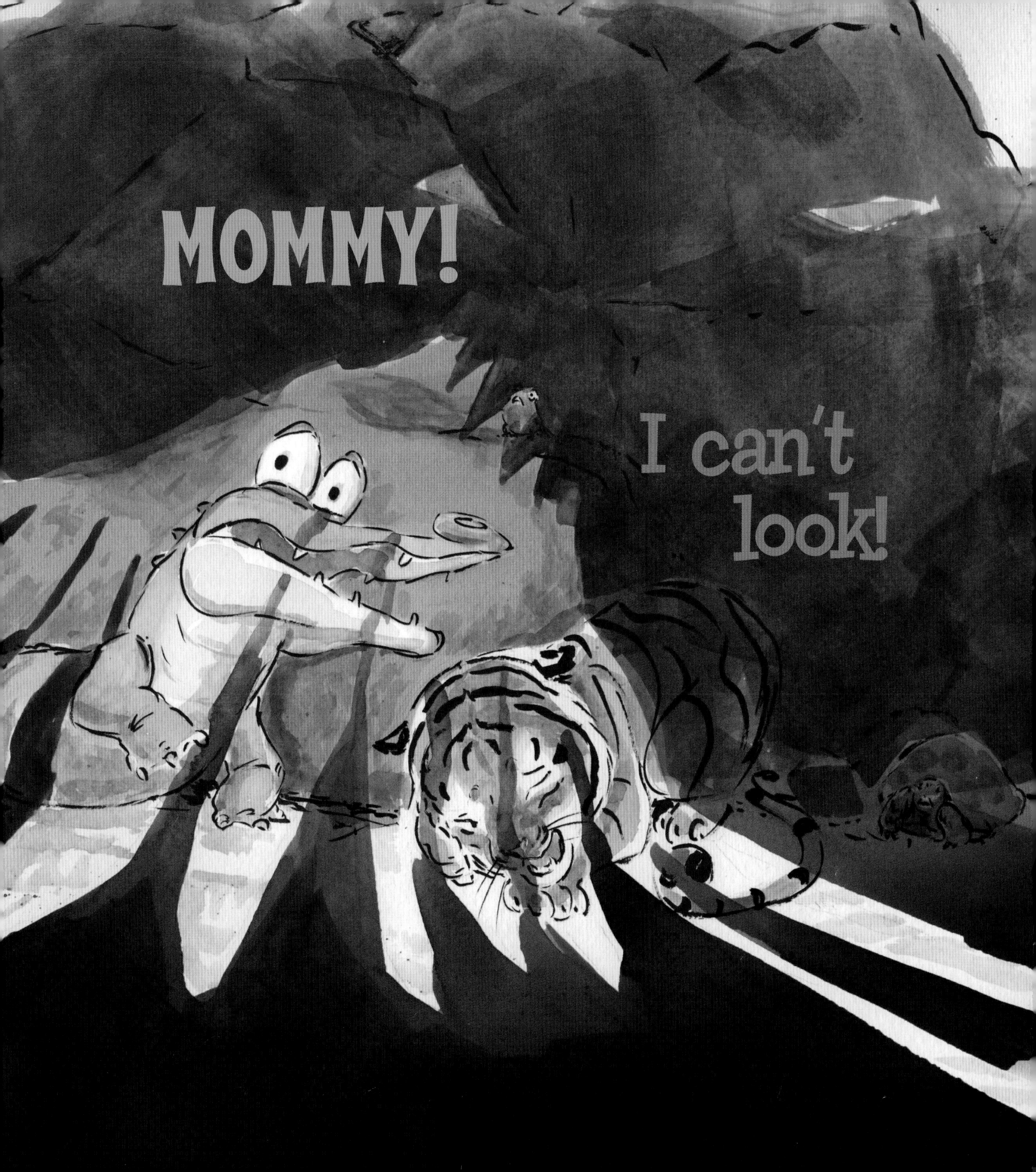

MOMMY!

I can't look!

There you two are.

We've been looking
all over for you.

Come on,
it's time to go home.

You know what?

What?

OUR MOMS are the scariest things in the jungle!

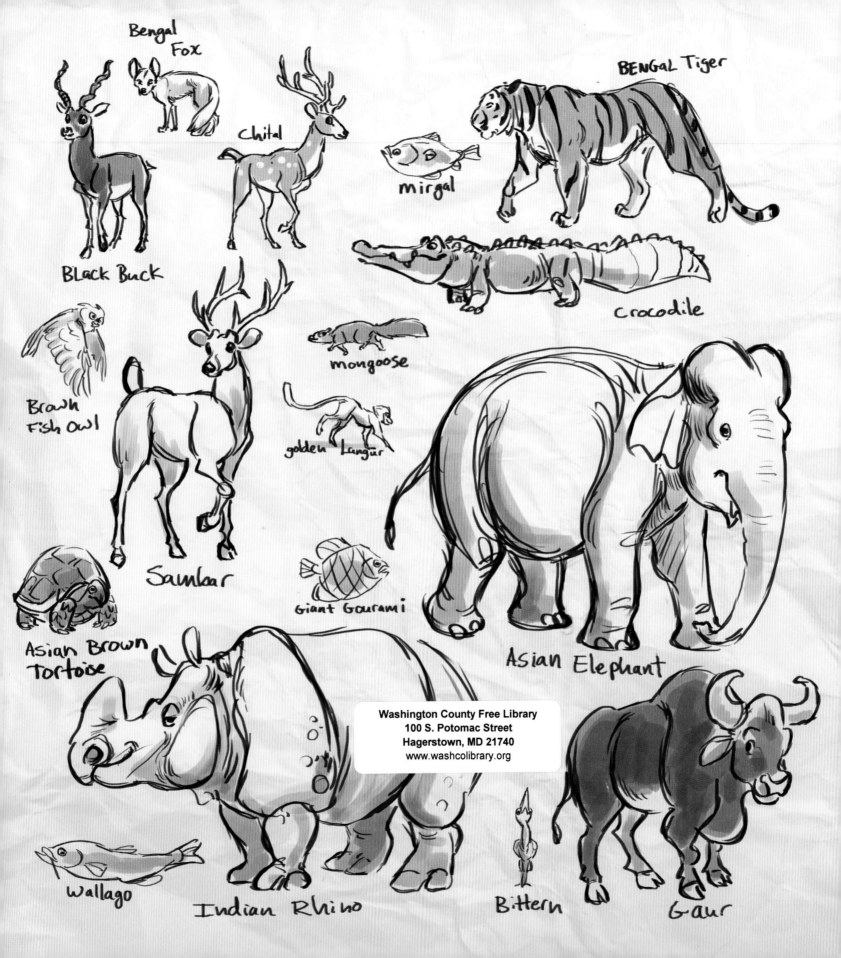

Bengal Fox

Chital

BENGAL Tiger

mirgal

Black Buck

crocodile

Brown Fish Owl

mongoose

Sambar

golden Langur

Asian Elephant

Giant Gourami

Asian Brown Tortoise

Wallago

Indian Rhino

Bittern

Gaur